CONTENTS

The Cuckoo in the Clock

and

Other Stories

by
Enid Blyton

Illustrated by
Lynne Byrnes

AWARD PUBLICATIONS

For further information on Enid Blyton please visit *www.blyton.com*

ISBN 978-1-84135-440-8

Illustrations copyright © Award Publications Limited

First published by Sampson Low as *Enid Blyton's Holiday Book Series*

This edition entitled *The Cuckoo in the Clock and Other Stories*
published by permission of Chorion Rights Limited

First published by Award Publications Limited 1994
This edition first published 2005

Published by Award Publications Limited,
The Old Riding School, The Welbeck Estate,
Worksop, Nottinghamshire, S80 3LR

09 3

Printed in the United Kingdom

The Cuckoo
in the Clock

There was a cuckoo-clock in the nursery. It was rather a fine one, made of wood, with carved leaves and flowers and birds all round it. At the top, in its tiny room, lived the wooden cuckoo. This room had a little door which flew open every half-hour – and out popped the cuckoo, bobbed and bowed, and cried "Cuckoo!" in a pretty voice.

All the toys liked the cuckoo. It was a nice, friendly little bird, and often asked the Noah's Ark animals to come and visit it. They were small enough to get inside the tiny room and have a talk. Sometimes the lion went up the chain to the cuckoo's little room, sometimes the kangaroo leapt up, and sometimes the bear went.

The cuckoo loved them all. One day the Noah's Ark ostrich brought some canary seed for the cuckoo to eat.

"I picked it up from the floor," said the ostrich. "The canary dropped it from her cage. You have it, Cuckoo, it will be a nice meal for you."

The cuckoo was grateful, though she didn't really like seed very much. She pecked at it and nibbled it – and almost forgot to pop out and say "Cuckoo!" at the right time.

Once, on a cold winter's day, the wooden cuckoo shivered in her tiny room. The cuckoo-clock was far away from the fire, and the nursery door was wide open.

"I shall be too cold to pop out and cry 'Cuckoo' at twelve o'clock!" thought the poor cuckoo. "I'm sure I'm getting a cold."

So she was, and her voice was so hoarse when she came out at twelve o'clock that all the toys were sorry for her.

"I'll climb up and give her a tiny

blanket off one of the cots in the dolls' house," said the toy clown. So up he went, carrying the little blanket in his pocket. He rapped on the cuckoo's door and she opened it.

"Here you are," said the clown, handing her the tiny blanket. "This will keep you warm, Cuckoo."

"Oh, thank you; you *are* kind to me!" cried the cuckoo gratefully. "This will wrap me up beautifully."

She wrapped the little cot blanket round her shoulders – and it *did* keep

7

her so nice and warm. When it was time for her to come out and cuckoo again, she quite forgot to take the blanket off her shoulders – and out she came with it round her!

The two children in the nursery did not notice, but all the toys did. They giggled among themselves and waited to see if the cuckoo would pop out with the blanket next time she cuckooed.

But this time she remembered to take it off. The toys were quite disappointed!

Once a dreadful thing happened. Somebody came to spring-clean the nursery, and they rubbed the cuckoo clock so hard that the door of the

8

cuckoo's room stuck fast and wouldn't open! The next time that the cuckoo wanted to come out and tell the time, she couldn't open her door!

So she stayed inside, frightened and silent, and the toys looked up in wonder. What had happened to the cuckoo?

All that day the cuckoo stayed in her little room inside the top of the clock, and didn't say a single cuckoo. The door stayed shut. The toys began to worry.

"Is the cuckoo ill, do you think?" said the clown. "We do miss her merry voice so much."

"We shan't know what the time is," said the baby-doll.

"Let's call up to her and see what has happened," said the pink rabbit.

So the clown stood below the clock and shouted loudly, "Cuckoo in the clock! Why don't you come out?"

All the answer they got was a tiny noise that sounded like someone doing their best to say "Cuckoo".

"I believe the door must be stuck,"

said the clown. "I'll go up and see."

So he climbed up the clock chains, and came to the cuckoo's door. Sure enough, it *was* stuck! The clown couldn't open it at all.

"I want a pin or something," he said. "Hie, Baby-doll, give me that brooch you wear – the one with 'BABY' on. That will open the door nicely."

"Oh, I can't lend you my brooch," said the baby-doll at once. She was very proud indeed of her lovely brooch. "You might break it."

"Baby-doll, how selfish you are!" cried the clown. "The poor cuckoo is locked in her room and can't ever get out unless you lend me your brooch to open the door."

"Oh, very well," said the baby-doll, who was really very fond of the cuckoo. She unfastened her beautiful brooch and threw it up to the clown. He caught it and began to dig into the door-catch with the pin of the brooch.

And at last he got the catch free so that the door would open once more. It

was just time for the cuckoo to cry eight o'clock, so she rushed out and called "Cuckoo" very loudly eight times. Everyone was delighted.

But alas for the baby-doll – the pin of the brooch was broken. The clown was very sorry.

"I couldn't help it," he said. "Don't make a fuss, Baby-doll. It was so kind of you to lend it."

The baby-doll didn't make a fuss, but

11

she went into a corner and cried by herself, because she had been very proud of the brooch. The cuckoo saw her crying there alone when she next popped out to cuckoo the half-hour, and she was very sorry.

"If only I could do something to show the baby-doll that I am grateful to her for lending her brooch to open my door!" she thought. "If only I could!"

Well, if anyone wants to repay a good turn they usually find a chance if they watch hard enough – and one day the cuckoo saw her chance.

She came out to cuckoo twelve o'clock one morning – and saw a wasp flying round the frightened baby-doll! "Help! Help!" squealed the doll. "It's going to sting me!"

All the toys were scared of wasps, and not even the clown dared to flap it away. It settled on the doll's pink cheek and she screamed.

"Now's my chance!" thought the cuckoo. And without thinking at all what she was doing, she flew straight

out of the clock, down to the baby-doll!

With her sharp wooden beak she pecked hard at the wasp. It gave an angry buzz and flew at the cuckoo. The cuckoo pecked at it again, and the wasp flew straight out of the window, buzzing, "I didn't know there was a bird in the nursery! I didn't know there was a bird in the nursery!"

"Oh, Cuckoo, you are wonderful!" cried the baby-doll. "Thank you so much. I really think I would have died of fright if you hadn't saved me from that wasp! How clever of you to fly right out of the clock! I didn't know you could."

"I didn't know I could, either," said the cuckoo, most surprised. "I say, Toys, isn't this wonderful! I'm out of the clock! I can come and play with you at night!"

So she can – and so she does. And sometimes the cuckoo-clock doesn't cuckoo at all in the night – not because it has stopped – oh no! But because the little wooden cuckoo is having a fine time playing with the toys. You should see her playing hide-and-seek – she cuckoos beautifully when she is hiding! Wouldn't I love to see her then!

Tubby
Makes a Mistake

"It's a very peculiar thing," said Mummy, looking into the biscuit jar, "but my biscuits do seem to be disappearing! Mandy – Harry – have you been taking any without asking?"

"Of course not!" said both children at once, and Mummy couldn't help thinking they were telling the truth. She knew, too, that they never took things that were not theirs to take. They were not that kind of children.

"Well, it's a puzzle," she said. "I know there was a chocolate biscuit in the jar yesterday, on the top of all the other biscuits – and now it isn't there! I can't imagine that it can be either of you children who has taken it. It would upset me very much."

The toys were sitting round the nursery and they heard all this. They looked at one another. No, it wasn't the children! The toys knew that. It was one of themselves!

The clown had distinctly heard somebody scrabbling in the biscuit jar up on the windowsill the night before. But it had been dark and he hadn't been able to see who it was. Still, he knew it was a toy.

16

"It's too bad that Mandy and Harry should be asked if they've taken the biscuits, when it's one of us toys," thought the clown. "We must really keep a watch and see who it is."

Now, it was Tubby, the bear, who had been taking biscuits whenever he could. He knew where they were kept – up on the windowsill, just behind the curtain. And each night, when the toys had crept into the toy cupboard, tired out with their playing, and had gone fast asleep, the greedy little bear had hauled himself up to the windowsill, taken off the lid of the jar, and put in his paw for a biscuit!

But that night, when the clown questioned everyone, he shook his little head with the others. "No," he said. "Dear me, no! I wouldn't *dream* of taking the biscuits."

"I'm not asking you if you'd *dream* about taking them. I'm asking you if you did *really* take them," said the clown, who wasn't very fond of Tubby.

"Of course I didn't taken them," said

Tubby most untruthfully. "I expect it was the mouse. Sure to be." Now the mouse was a great friend of all the toys, and was a gentle, honest little creature that would not even take a crumb from the floor without asking the clown's permission. The toys frowned when they heard Tubby say it was the mouse.

"You mustn't accuse other people of doing things unless you have certain proof," said the clown sternly. "Just because the mouse is fond of biscuits doesn't mean that he would steal some."

Tubby didn't take any biscuits that night. He had an idea that the clown was trying to keep awake and listen to see if anyone was scrabbling about in the biscuit jar again. So he sat quietly in his corner and did nothing.

But the next night he kept on and on thinking of the biscuits in that jar. He knew the children's mother had filled up the jar that morning – there would be heaps of delicious biscuits there! He must get one, he really must!

He listened hard. He couldn't hear a sound in the nursery at all. All the toys had been playing very wild games that night and they were tired out. Everyone was fast asleep.

Tubby could be very quiet when he wanted to. He stood up. He caught hold of the long curtain and hauled himself up to the window-seat, and then to the sill. Ah, there was the biscuit jar, in its usual place. Good!

Very, very quietly he lifted off the lid. He put in a fat paw. He felt a biscuit at once, because the jar was quite full. He took it out and put back the lid. He didn't make the very slightest noise.

He slid down to the floor again. He nibbled the biscuit for a long time and enjoyed it. Then he thought of something very naughty. He ran quietly to the little hole where the mouse came out to play, and he put down a few biscuit crumbs there. Now the toys would think it was the mouse who took the biscuits!

In the morning Mummy noticed that another biscuit had gone. She was vexed. "It was a pink wafer – one that was right on the top," she said. "It

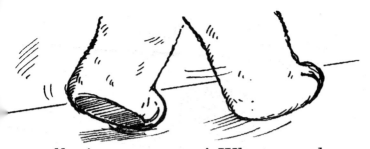

really is a mystery! What can have happened to it?"

When the nursery was empty, the toy cat spoke up. "Golly," she said, "I see crumbs – biscuit crumbs!"

"Where?" said all the toys.

"At the entrance of the mousehole," said the toy cat. Everyone stared at them. Oh dear! Could it really be the gentle little mouse who was the thief?

"I shall really have to find out," thought the clown with a sigh. "I must set a trap. It's a horrid thing to do, but it's even horrider to have a thief in our midst and not know who it is."

But he didn't know what trap to set. And then he suddenly thought of something! The mistletoe was still hanging up, for it hadn't yet been taken down, as Christmas was only just over.

21

One of the berries dropped from it and the clown accidentally trod on it.

It stuck to his foot. He simply could *not* shake it off. Mistletoe berries are very, very sticky, and this one seemed almost as if it was glued to his foot.

That gave him a good idea. "I know what I'll do," he said to himself. "I'll get some of these sticky berries, and I'll put them on the windowsill, just by the biscuit jar. The thief will go there in the dark, and perhaps he will tread on them. Then tomorrow morning I'll look at everyone's feet, and whoever has got berries squashed underneath their feet will be the thief. How clever I am!"

It was rather difficult to get up to the mistletoe, but he managed it. The toys were surprised to see the clown picking a spray of leaves and berries. He didn't tell them why, of course. He just put the spray in a little vase in the dolls' house, and everyone thought it was instead of flowers.

But that night, whilst all the toys were playing "touch-me-last", the

clown slipped up to the windowsill. Yes, there was the biscuit jar as usual! The clown pulled the sticky grey-green berries off the mistletoe spray and pressed them lightly on the windowsill, near the biscuit jar. Then he slid down to the floor.

Nobody saw him. They were all too busy playing, even Tubby, the bear. They played till they were tired out. Then they went into the toy cupboard to sleep. The dolls put themselves back into their beds or cots, the bricks hopped into their box, the other toys just flopped down into corners.

The bear went to his corner, too. He was tired, but he couldn't help thinking of those lovely biscuits in the jar. He must, he simply *must* get one! It wouldn't take a minute. Then he could sit and nibble it in comfort.

He hauled himself up by the curtain. It was very, very dark now, and he couldn't see the jar on the windowsill. He had to feel about for it. Ah – there it was! But dear me, a good many of the biscuits had been eaten, and the bear had to put his arm right inside the jar to find a biscuit for himself. He sat down on the windowsill, leaned over the jar and began to feel about for a biscuit.

He didn't know that he had sat on all the sticky berries. He didn't know that they were sticking fast to him. He didn't guess about the clown's trick at all. No – he got himself a biscuit, put on the lid again and slid down to the floor, the squashed berries sticking to him very tightly indeed!

He ate the biscuit. Then he fell asleep. In the morning, what a to-do! Another biscuit gone!

"Really!" said Mummy. "I shall have to set a policeman to guard our biscuits. WHO is taking them?"

The clown looked round at all the toys. He could see the feet of some of them, for they were sitting down on the floor. The big doll had no berries under her feet. The toy cat had none. She was lying down and the clown could see the soles of all four of her feet.

He looked at the bear. Tubby was sitting down against the wall, his fat hind paws turned up. He had no sticky berries on his feet either. Who had?

When Mandy and Harry had gone for a walk, and the nursery was empty, the clown spoke sternly. "I want to see everyone's feet, please!"

The toys looked at him in surprise and alarm. Why did he speak like that? One by one they walked over to him, Tubby too, and showed him their feet. But not one of the toys had the sticky berries squashed beneath them. How strange!

But just then Tubby turned his back

26

to walk away – and the clown looked at him in astonishment. Why – why – Tubby had sticky berries on his little sit-me-down! He had! No doubt about it at all.

"Tubby!" said the clown in such a very stern voice that Tubby jumped. "Have you been stealing the biscuits?"

"Certainly not," said Tubby, but he couldn't help his face going red.

All the toys came round. The clown took hold of Tubby and turned him round so that the toys could see where the mistletoe berries had stuck.

"Look, toys!" he said. "Isn't this a peculiar thing – poor old Tubby has sat on some nasty sticky berries – and do

you know, toys, those berries were up on the windowsill beside the biscuit jar? What do you make of *that*?"

"Now, look here!" said Tubby in a loud, blustery, growly voice. "I've not taken the biscuits – you know very well the mouse took them. Didn't you see the crumbs in his hole?"

"The mouse has gone to see his aunt in the fields," said the clown sternly. "He hasn't been here for at least three nights. Tubby, I don't know which is worse, do you; – to steal biscuits, or to say the mouse took them when he didn't?"

"Well, I didn't take them," said Tubby, looking very bold still. "And don't you dare to try and punish me, clown!"

"Oh no! Oh, dear me, no!" said the clown in a polite voice. "But really, we must try and get those sticky berries off you, Tubby. It must be most uncomfortable for you to keep sitting down on them. I'll hold you, and the toys can try and get them off."

He caught hold of Tubby – and then, good gracious me, what a dreadful time poor Tubby had! The toys knew quite well he had been very naughty indeed, and you should have seen them try to get off those berries! They slapped the bear, they smacked at those berries, they banged them, they hit them hard – but the sticky berries wouldn't be shaken off!

Tubby yelled and howled and wriggled. "Stand still – we've nearly got one berry off!" said the clown. "That's right, sailor doll – give another good whack!"

Smack, slap, biff, whack!

"You're hurting me, you're hitting *me*, not the berries!" howled Tubby. But he had to be punished, and a very good thing it was, too.

"There! All the berries are off now, and you can sit down in comfort," said the clown. But Tubby couldn't sit down at all. He went and stood in a corner, hid his face in his hands and wept.

"I did take the biscuits," he sobbed.

"Don't punish me any more. I did take them!"

"I know," said the clown. "I laid a little trap for you, Tubby. And I wouldn't have let everyone be so rough with you if you hadn't said that our friend the mouse had taken them. You deserved all you got!"

Tubby never took a biscuit again. And he hates to see mistletoe put up now at Christmas time, because of those sticky berries! Did you know they were so sticky? Squash one in your fingers and see!

31

The Big
Glass Marble

Every boy in the school had his own marbles – but Benny had the biggest one. I wish you could have seen that marble! It was as big as a small ball, and inside it were curly streaks of green, blue, red and yellow.

It was made of glass, so you could see right to the middle of it. Benny was very, very proud of it. He showed it to everyone at least twice a day, and though John offered his twelve small marbles for it, he wouldn't part with that fine marble.

The school was at the top of the hill. Every day the children had to climb up to it. Benny used to put his hand in his pocket and feel his big marble every time he went to school. Mummy said he was quite silly about it!

"You treat that marble as if it was a pet dog or something," Mummy said. "I'm surprised you don't buy it a bone, or give it a drink of milk!"

"I love it best of anything I've got," said Benny.

Now one day the boys went out to play in the playground of the school and they had a game of "Touch". Harry tore after Benny, and Benny ran away shouting. He fell over with a bang and his marble flew out of his pocket! Benny had hurt both his knees badly, and he was so worried about them that for a minute or two he didn't notice that his marble was gone.

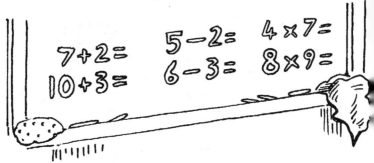

Then, when his knees were bound up with his hanky and Harry's, he felt for his marble to make sure it was safe. Just suppose it was broken!

It wasn't in his pocket! It was gone! Benny began to look for it. "I say!" he said. "My marble's gone. You know – that lovely big one of mine. Help me to look for it."

Well, everyone hunted till the bell rang for them to go back to lessons again, but nobody could find it. They hunted in every single corner of the playground, but it wasn't there. Benny was so upset that he nearly cried, but he didn't quite. He couldn't do his sums properly because he kept thinking about the marble. He couldn't do his

34

geography. Mr Brown got really cross. But it was no good, Benny couldn't think of anything but his beautiful lost marble.

And now what had happened to his marble? Well, I'll tell you!

When Benny had fallen down, that marble had shot straight out of his pocket to the ground. It had rolled to the gate, and had slipped under it. There it was, at the top of the hill. Well, of course you know what all marbles and balls do on a hill – they roll down!

So the marble began to roll downhill. It was very pleased. It liked an adventure. It was tired of being in Benny's pocket and being held in his

hot hand. It wanted to run around and see people.

So down the hill it went. Soon it came to a party of sparrows in the gutter, quarrelling over some bread. It rolled up to them and they looked at it in surprise.

"What are you?" asked a sparrow.

"I'm the great big Rollaby-Roo," said the marble grandly, making up the name just that minute.

"What do you eat?" asked the sparrow, hoping that the Rollaby-Roo didn't peck bread.

"I eat chimney pots and apple pips," said the marble, most untruthfully. The sparrows stared at him in surprise. It seemed a funny sort of mixture.

The marble had run into a little hole in the road, and he stayed there, quite still. The sparrows thought he might be going to eat their bread after all, as there didn't seem to be any chimney pots and apple pips nearby for him to peck. So one of them pecked him hard – and that set him rolling down the hill again!

"Goodbye!" he said. "I'm off on my adventures again!"

Soon he came to where a kitten played in the road with a bit of paper. The kitten stared at the marble, who stopped nearby.

"Who are you?" asked the kitten.

"I'm the great big Slip-Along-Shiny," said the marble grandly.

"Good gracious!" said the kitten. "Where do you live?"

"Oh, sometimes in teapots and sometimes in worm holes!" said the marble naughtily. He really was enjoying himself. The kitten laughed. She patted him with her paw and sent him rolling quickly down the hill again.

"Well, go and find a teapot or a worm hole!" she mewed.

Off went the marble, rolling down the road. Presently he came to where a big brown horse stood, waiting for his master to come out from a shop. The marble bumped into one of the horse's hoofs and stopped. The horse looked down and saw him.

"Who are you?" said the horse in surprise.

"Oh, I'm the Rumble-Rattle-Roarer," said the marble, thinking how clever he was at names.

"Never heard of you before," said the horse. "Where do you come from?"

"I come from the egg of an elephant!" said the untruthful marble with a giggle.

38

"Elephants don't lay eggs!" snorted the horse, and he kicked the marble with his hoof. It rolled down the hill again. What an adventure this was!

It rolled down for a very long way, and didn't meet anyone at all. Then it met a dog, sniffing about the gutter. The marble rolled into his nose and the dog jumped back in fright.

"Who's this?" he wuffed.

"It's the Thingummy-Jig!" cried the marble. "Haven't you ever heard of the Thingummy-Jig?"

"I don't think so," said the dog. "Who is your master?"

"My master is the Man in the Moon," giggled the marble. The dog nosed him out of the gutter and he went off down the hill again, rolling, rolling, rolling.

He felt tired. He had come a very long way. He had had a lot of adventures. Now he longed for Benny's warm pocket. He rolled on and on, and at last came to a gateway. He rolled inside the gate and down the garden path.

"I wish I was with Benny now," he said to himself. "I'm tired of adventures!"

Where *was* Benny? Well, he had looked for his marble again after school and hadn't found it. He had been very unhappy. He went home down the hill, and his right-hand pocket felt strangely empty. There was no big glass marble there!

He went indoors to tell his mother all about how he had lost it. She was very, very sorry.

"Don't worry about it, Benny," she said. "It may turn up. Things do sometimes, when they are lost."

"Oh, Mummy, that marble will never turn up again," said Benny. "It's lost forever."

Then suddenly his mother caught hold of his arm and pointed out of the window – and whatever *do* you think Benny saw? Yes – he saw his lovely glass marble rolling slowly in at the gate! It rolled to the front door and stopped. It could go no further, for the step was there.

"My marble! My fine glass marble!" cried Benny, and he rushed to get it. "So you came home after all! You clever, clever thing!"

"Dear me, I really am very, very clever," thought the marble in surprise. "I didn't know this was Benny's house – but it is."

So after that it felt grander than ever, and you should just have heard the way it told the other marbles all its wonderful adventures! No wonder they jiggle and giggle together in Benny's pocket.

The Strange
Sailor Doll

One day Peter came to tea with Jill. He had with him a sailor doll, but neither Jill nor Peter played with him. It was much more fun playing with all Jill's exciting toys. She had such a lot, because she had plenty of aunts and uncles, and they gave her toys whenever they came to see her.

Peter liked best of all a little motor-car. It ran very fast across the room when it was wound up, and it had a little hooter that tooted loudly every now and again, all by itself. Peter thought it was wonderful.

"Oh, Jill, I do wish you'd give me this," he kept saying. "I never in my life saw such a dear little car – and the way it hoots, too! Honestly, I'd just love to have it for my own. Do give it to me."

"You're not supposed to ask for other people's toys when you go out to tea," said Jill.

"I know," said Peter. "I know quite well it isn't polite. But I can't help it this time. I say – suppose I give you my sailor doll? Would you exchange this little car for him?"

"Well, I don't much want him," said Jill, looking at the doll. "He seems rather ordinary to me. And why ever does he wear gloves?"

"Does he? Well, I never noticed it!" said Peter. "Perhaps Mummy made him a pair sometime. Oh, do let me give him to you for this car."

"All right," said Jill. "I don't really want him – but then, I don't really want the car either. I've got three others. Take it, and leave the sailor doll."

And that was how Sailor came to live in Jill's house. The other toys crowded round him that night when Jill had gone to sleep. He looked shyly at them.

"I hope you don't mind me coming here," he said. "I'm sorry to leave Peter, really – though he isn't very good with his toys, you know. I like the look of your Jill."

"She's nice," said Angela, the big doll. "Sailor, why do you wear gloves? Take them off. They look silly when you are indoors."

The sailor doll went rather red. "I don't take them off even when I'm indoors," he said. "I'd rather not, thank you."

45

The toys laughed. "Why? Are your hands cold?" said the ragdoll. "Poor boy! His hands are cold, so he wears gloves! Ho, ho, ho!"

Sailor soon settled down among the toys. He seemed shy and didn't join in their games very much. The big brown teddy bear teased him about it.

"Hey, Sailor! Why don't you come and play head-over-heels tonight? Come on! And we're going to play leapfrog too!"

"I don't think I will, thank you," said the sailor doll, politely.

46

"He's afraid of getting his gloves dirty!" laughed the teddy bear. "Take off your gloves, Sailor – yes, and your coat too – and come and play properly. You're always so dressed up and polite."

But Sailor wouldn't. He went red and walked away to a corner by himself, where he talked to the clockwork mouse, who was timid and shy too.

The toys grew rather impatient with him. He had such a jolly face, and yet he wouldn't be jolly. But they were more impatient than ever one night when he wouldn't join in with their work. They wanted to build a ladder of bricks right up to the windowsill, so that they could climb up and look out.

"Come on, Sailor – do your share!" shouted the ragdoll, impatiently. "Take off your coat and help us. Keep your silly gloves on if you want to – but you'll be awfully hot if you work in your coat, because these bricks are jolly heavy."

"If you don't mind, I don't think I will help with the building," said Sailor.

"Why not? Are you afraid of hard work?" asked the ragdoll.

"No," said Sailor.

"He's bone-lazy," said Angela, the big doll. "Aren't you, Sailor? Too lazy to play and too lazy to work."

"It's a pity he came to our house," said the bear. "He's no good at all. Won't join in anything. He's lazy and stupid, and I expect he's a little coward too. Let's not have anything more to do with him."

So after that they didn't speak to Sailor, and he might not have been in the room at all. Only the clockwork mouse spoke to him, and that was brave of him because he knew the others didn't like him for it.

Now, one day Mummy spoke to Jill, and the toys heard what she said. She said: "Jill, will you put all your oldest toys in this basket, because I'll give them away to Mrs Brown. She has eleven children, and they hardly have any toys."

"All right, Mummy," said Jill, and went to her toy cupboard. She took out some bricks, a ball that had a hole in it, an old kite, a train that hadn't any lines, and some other things she never played with.

49

When she had put them all into the basket and gone out of the room, the toys looked at one another. "I'm glad *I* wasn't put into the basket," said the bear. "I've heard that Mrs Brown's children are rough and rude. I wouldn't like to be one of *their* toys."

"Nor would I," said Sailor.

"We're not speaking to you, so please don't speak to us," snapped the ragdoll.

"It's a pity you weren't put into the basket, because you're not really wanted here," said Angela, unkindly.

"Very well. I'll put myself in!" said poor Sailor, looking as if he were going to burst into tears.

"Do – gloves and all!" said the ragdoll in a very nasty voice. The sailor doll walked over to the basket of old toys and set himself on the top of them, looking very, very miserable.

"You won't be much loss," said Angela. "Stuck-up thing, never taking your gloves off, or even your coat, to play our games or help in our work."

Sailor said nothing at all. The

clockwork mouse went and sat beside the basket to show Sailor he still had one friend, but he didn't dare to say anything to him. Still, Sailor was very thankful to see him there. It made him feel a little less lonely.

Suddenly the door opened and in came Jill with Peter. He had come to borrow a book. He carried with him a beautiful toy horse with a real furry coat. He set it down on the floor while he went to look in Jill's bookcase.

All the toys gazed in delight at the toy horse. He was lovely, really lovely. His tail was long and swishy, his ears were cocked up, and his mane was beautiful. He had a little white mark on his brown nose, and bright eyes which looked all round the big room.

"Isn't he magnificent?" whispered

Angela to the teddy bear. "I've never seen a toy horse as grand as he is before!"

"I wish we could talk to him," whispered back the bear. "But we daren't while Jill and Peter are in the room."

Well, would you believe it, when Peter found a book to take home with him, he went out of the room with Jill and quite forgot to take his horse with him. There he stood on the floor, looking very handsome and proud.

The toys went across to him. "I say! Aren't you fine?" said the bear. "Let me stroke your coat. It's real hair! And your tail is wonderful. Swish it about."

The horse swished it, and then he kicked up his heels and galloped round and round the room, neighing in a high little horse-voice.

"Oh! You're grand!" cried all the toys, and even the clockwork mouse squeaked in delight. Then suddenly the little toy horse came to a stop and looked all round. "I say!" he said. "I've just remembered something. Haven't you got a friend of mine here, Sailor Doll? Didn't Peter give him to Jill in exchange for a little motor-car that hooted?"

"Yes," said Angela, the big doll. "Was he really a friend of yours? How strange! We simply can't bear him and his silly ways. Why, he always wears gloves, and he won't even take off his coat to do anything, work or play!"

"Did you ever bother to find out why?" said the little horse, swishing his tail. "No, I can see you didn't. Where is Sailor? I simply must go and say how-do-you-do to him! He's a grand fellow!"

The toys were most astonished to hear this. Angela waved to the basket of old toys. "He's over there, with the old toys that are going to be given away."

The horse galloped up to the basket. He put his front hoofs up on to the tip of the basket and looked inside. "Hrrrrrrrumph!" he said. "Hey, Sailor! Don't you remember Dobbin, the horse in Peter's room? You often used to ride me."

Sailor stood up, his face shining. "Oh, *Dobbin*! It's really you! How is everyone at Peter's?"

"Come out of the basket and I'll tell you all the news," said the little horse. "Get on to my back – that's right – and we'll have a little trot together."

The toys watched Dobbin trotting round the room with Sailor on his back. Sailor looked very, very happy. When the ride was over, he leapt off and stroked Dobbin's white-starred nose.

"How's your arm, old fellow?" said

56

Dobbin. "Got a new one yet? Does it hurt much?"

"Not much," said Sailor. "No, I haven't got a new one, and I'm afraid I never shall."

"What's the matter with his arm?" said the bear suddenly, walking up.

"Nothing much," said Sailor, turning away.

"*I'll* tell you," said the horse, suddenly. "I'll tell you quite a lot – and I hope you'll be ashamed when I've finished, you unkind toys!"

"No, don't tell them," begged Sailor. "I never tell anyone."

"You're too modest," said the horse. "Listen, toys. When Sailor was in Peter's room, a puppy came gambolling into the room one day. He pounced on our baby doll and threw her up into the air. She screamed like anything. Well, when she fell to the floor, Sailor rushed over and flung himself on top of her so that the puppy couldn't get her again."

"Go on," said Angela. "Tell us the rest."

"Well," went on the little horse, "the puppy was angry, but Sailor wouldn't move – and he lay there, protecting the baby doll, and he let the puppy chew his right arm off!"

Angela screamed. The other toys exclaimed loudly. Sailor went very red.

"But – he's got two arms," squeaked the clockwork mouse.

"Oh no, he hasn't," said the toy

58

horse. "Sailor, take off your coat. Go on – let them see. It's time they knew all this!"

Sailor took off his coat, and the toys looked at him in sad surprise. He had one good arm – but the other was just a piece of stick, glued on to his shoulder!

"Peter's mother glued it on," said the horse. "She didn't tell Peter about it in case he beat the puppy. And she made Sailor a tiny pair of gloves so that nobody would notice one of his hands was only the end of a stick. I tell you, Sailor is a grand fellow, one of my best friends – and if anyone wants to say a word against him, just let them say it here and now! I'll kick them up to the ceiling!"

But nobody wanted to say a word against Sailor. Everyone was ashamed and sad. They all went as red as beetroots, even the ragdoll, and that was difficult for him because he had quite a red face already.

The bear went up to Sailor and held out his paw.

"Sorry, Sailor," he said. "Please forgive me. I should have guessed all this."

Sailor shook hands with his proper hand, and grinned happily. "It's all right. I got all funny about my arm. I just felt I couldn't tell anyone it was just a stick."

"Don't you wear your gloves any more," begged Angela, and she hugged him. "We shan't mind your stick-arm a bit. We shall be proud of you whenever we see it!"

Sailor was so happy that he just stood there and smiled all over his face. Everyone came and shook hands with him and said they were sorry, would he be friends with them? Sailor put on his coat again – but he threw the gloves into the pile of old toys in the basket. "Shan't wear those any more!" he said. "Listen – here come Peter and Jill again – we must be quiet."

"They've remembered me and come to fetch me," said the little toy horse. "Goodbye, Sailor. I'm glad I came today and put things right for you."

Peter and Jill came in, and Peter picked up his horse. "Hallo, there's old Sailor," he said. "He looks very happy. Hello, Sailor! How nice to see you again!"

Sailor felt happier than ever. When Jill and Peter had gone out of the room

again, he turned head-over-heels twice, just to show the toys that he didn't care about his silly old stick-arm any more.

"Be careful!" said Angela, in alarm. "You'll break it. Oh – I've got such a good idea!"

"What?" cried everyone.

"Well, I know where there's a box that Jill's Mummy keeps, with all sorts of odds and ends in," said Angela. "And I do believe there's an old arm there

that once belonged to a broken doll.
Couldn't we find it and put it on Sailor?
It would be a bit shorter than his own,
but that wouldn't matter a bit!"

So they are going to find it tonight
and put it on for him. Sailor's so excited
and happy that he doesn't know what
to do. "To think I nearly went away
with the old toys to Mrs Brown's
children!" he keeps saying. "Well, well –
you simply never know what's going to
happen!"

The Toy Clown
and the Radio

There was a new radio in the playroom.
It had only just arrived, and the two
children were excited about it.

"You just turn that knob there, and
the music plays," said Betty.

"You can turn it if you like," said
Mummy. So Betty turned it, very slowly,
and to the great astonishment of the
toys, a band began to play out of the
radio. The clown looked at it in great
surprise. The teddy bear almost fell off
the shelf, and the yellow cat was really
frightened.

"Isn't it lovely?" said John. "May
Betty and I have it on whenever we
like, Mummy?"

"Yes – but not too loudly," said
Mummy. "You must remember there

are plenty of other people around, and they don't want to have to hear your radio all the time."

The toys thought the radio was really wonderful. They were never tired of listening to it. Sometimes people spoke out of the radio, and the toys wondered how they got there. Sometimes people played the piano in the radio, and that seemed wonderful too. How could a piano get into that small radio?

At night, when the children had gone to bed, the clown looked longingly at the radio.

"It's magic," he said to the others. "It must be magic. How else can it have bands and things inside it? I wish I could open it and see exactly what is inside. How do you suppose you open it, Teddy?"

"Don't *think* of such a thing!" cried the bear in horror. "You might break it."

"I must just peep inside and see," said the clown, and he began to try and

66

undo a screw at the back. The bear had to get the big sailor doll to come and help him take the clown away.

"We shall put you inside the brick box, if you don't solemnly promise you won't try to see inside the radio," said the teddy bear. The clown didn't at all want to be put into the brick box, because there was so little room there, so he had to promise.

The next night he wanted to turn the knob that made the radio play. "I want to see the light come on, and hear the music," he said. "*Just* let me turn the knob!"

"What! Wake up everyone in the house and have them rushing to the room to see what's the matter?" cried the teddy bear. "You must be mad."

"Would they hear it?" said the clown. "Oh, do let me try. I'll only turn the knob a tiny way then the music won't be very loud."

"You really are very, very naughty, clown," said the bear. "You are not to turn the knob at all."

The clown was quite good for a night or two, and then, when the toys were playing quietly in a corner, he crept over to the radio and turned the knob. The light shone inside the radio set, and a band began to play!

It was true that the music was very quiet indeed, but all the same, the toys were quite horrified! The bear and the sailor doll rushed over at once and turned off the knob. The light went out. The music stopped.

"Clown! How dare you!" cried the teddy bear. "Are you quite, quite mad? Do you want to wake up the whole family?"

"No – and anyway the music played

itself so quietly that nobody would have heard it," said the clown. "It is you, with your big shouting voice, that will wake up everyone! Be quiet. You are not to shout at me."

"Shall we put him in the brick box?" said the sailor doll.

"You shan't, you shan't!" said the clown, and he ran away. He squeezed himself under the nursery piano, and nobody could get him out.

"Very well. Stay there!" said the bear. "We shan't talk to you or play with you. You are a very bad toy."

69

So nobody spoke to the clown that night, not even the little clockwork mouse, who loved to chatter to him. It was very sad. Nobody asked him to join in the games, and the clown felt very lonely indeed.

The next night it was just the same. The clown asked the bear to play catch, but the bear just looked at him and walked away. Then the clown spoke to the baby doll.

"How the moon shines tonight!" he said. But the baby doll stared at him with her big blue eyes and didn't answer a word.

The clown was offended. He walked away. "Very well!" he called, over his shoulder. "If you won't play with me I'm going out of the room! I won't stay with such horrid toys!"

So out of the nursery door he went, whilst all the toys stared after him in horror. No toy ever went out of the playroom at night. Whatever was the clown thinking of to do such a thing?

The moon shone brightly, and the

clown could see quite plainly where he was going. He went down the stairs, jumping them one at a time. They seemed very, very steep to him! He got down to the bottom, and looked round. He had sometimes been taken downstairs by Betty. He knew there was a room called the kitchen that had a nice smell in it. Which was it?

He found the kitchen door and sidled round it. The kitchen was bright in the

moonlight, and the pots and pans winked and blinked.

"There may be a crumb or two on the floor," thought the clown, and he began to look under the table. Suddenly a shadow fell across the moonlit floor, and the clown looked up in surprise. Had the moon gone behind a cloud?

No, it hadn't. Somebody had put himself in front of the moon – and that somebody was getting in at the kitchen window! The clown stared in the greatest surprise. Who was this, forcing open the kitchen window in the middle of the night, and getting inside?

72

"It must be a burglar!" thought the clown in dismay. "They come in the night sometimes, and steal things. Oh, whatever shall I do? My voice isn't big enough to wake everyone up. Oh dear, oh dear, what shall I do?"

The burglar sprang quietly to the floor, and opened the larder door. He meant to have something to eat. The clown scuttled out of the kitchen as fast as his little legs would take him. The burglar saw him in the moonlight and jumped.

"What's that? A rat, I suppose?" he thought.

But it wasn't a rat. It was a frightened clown, hurrying upstairs as fast as he could go, climbing one step at a time. He came to the playroom and rushed round the door, panting. The toys looked at him in amazement.

"Goodness! What's the matter? Your face is quite pale!"

"It's a burglar, a burglar! Downstairs in the kitchen!" cried the clown. "We must wake everyone up! Oh, quick, quick, make a noise, everyone."

The teddy bear growled. The baby doll said "Ma-ma, Ma-ma!" The pink cat squeaked, and so did the clown. The sailor doll rapped on the floor. But it was no good. No one heard them. No one woke up.

And then the clown did a most peculiar thing! He gave a little cry, and rushed over to the radio set. He turned on the knob – turned it right round as far as it would go! The light went on inside the set – and, dear me, what a tremendous noise came blaring forth!

It was a man's voice, telling the midnight news; but the clown had put the radio on so loudly that it was as if the man on the wireless was shouting at the top of his voice.

"You bad clown!" cried the bear, and ran to turn it off. But the clown pushed him away.

"Don't! I'm waking up the household!

I'm not naughty this time, I'm good."

And so he was – for the shouting on the radio woke up everyone with a jump. It frightened the burglar in the kitchen, and he knocked over some saucepans with a clatter. Daddy ran downstairs with a poker, and saw the burglar crouching in the larder. Quick as lightning Daddy shut the door and locked it. The burglar was a prisoner!

Then upstairs went Daddy to see what the shouting was in the playroom. He found Betty and John just turning off the radio there.

"This is what woke us up, Daddy," said John. "The radio. But who could have put it on?"

Nobody knew. Betty caught a gleam in the clown's eye, as he sat by the toy cupboard. Could *he* possibly have turned on the radio? Betty knew quite well she had put him back into the toy cupboard that evening – and there he was, sitting outside it! She felt sure he had been up to something!

The policemen came and collected

the burglar out of the larder. Everyone went back to bed. The toys came out of the toy cupboard, dancing about in glee.

"The burglar's caught! Good old clown!"

"You've been so good and clever that we'll forget you were naughty before!"

"*What* a noise the radio made, didn't it!"

The clown was pleased to find himself such a hero. He beamed all over his face. "Now listen to me," he said, "whenever I want to turn the radio on at night *ever* so quietly you're to let me! I won't wake anyone at all. But I'm GOING TO TURN IT ON WHEN I WANT TO!"

"All right," said the bear. "We shan't stop you, you deserve a little reward. You really have been very, very clever."

Everyone agreed, and the clockwork mouse felt very proud of his friend.

And now when he feels like a little music the clown turns the radio knob – very gently – and the music comes whispering out. Betty and John *will* be surprised if they hear it, won't they?

The Doll That
Fell out of the Pram

Once there was a doll who fell out of her pram. She belonged to Joanna and Joanna was taking her for a walk. She was with Sarah, and both little girls had their dolls' prams with them.

"I shall sit Angela up for a while," said Joanna, and she sat Angela right up. But Sarah let her doll Rosie lie down. She said she had not had enough sleep yet.

The little girls were going up a hill. "Oh, it's hard work pushing the prams," said Joanna. "Let's *pull* them behind us, instead of pushing."

So they walked up the hill pulling their prams behind them, their backs to the dolls, talking away hard.

Joanna's pram went over a stone.

Angela, the doll, was jerked up in the air. She fell across the side of the pram, tried to save herself, and then slipped right over in the road. Joanna and Sarah didn't see or hear what had happened. They went on talking and walking up the hill.

The doll lay in the lane. Hardly anyone came down that lane, so Angela was not likely to be found. She was very frightened. When anyone pressed her middle she could squeal, so she pressed her tummy with her little hands, and squealed very loudly indeed.

"Eeee, eeee, eee, eee! Eeee, eee, ee, ee!"

A rabbit heard her and peeped through the hedge in surprise. A blackbird heard her and flew down. A hedgehog wondered what the noise was and scurried up to see. They were all astonished to find Angela squeaking by herself in the lane.

"What's the matter?" they asked.

"Eee, eee – I fell out of the pram!" squealed Angela.

"Well, run after it," said the rabbit.

"Fly after it," said the blackbird.

"Scurry!" said the hedgehog.

"Eee, ee, I can't walk," said poor Angela. "My legs won't move by themselves."

"Stand her up," said the rabbit. So they stood Angela up, but she at once fell down again, and almost choked the blackbird, because she fell on his neck.

"Let's take her to the pram ourselves," said the rabbit. "I'll take her hair and pull her."

"I'll take a bit of her dress in my mouth and fly with her," said the blackbird.

"I'll get underneath and push," said the hedgehog.

But Angela didn't enjoy that at all. "You're pulling my hair!" she squeaked to the rabbit. "You're tearing my dress!" she cried to the blackbird. "You're pricking me!" she shouted to the hedgehog. "Eeee, eee, eee!"

Then down flew a small pixie, in the greatest surprise. "Now what are you doing, hurting that poor doll?" she cried crossly. "Leave her alone!"

"We're trying to help her," said the rabbit, offended. "She's fallen out of her pram."

"Well, let her walk after it," said the pixie.

"I *can't!*" wept Angela, and she pressed herself in the tummy so hard that she almost broke her squeak. "EEEEEEEE!"

"My goodness, what a voice!" said the pixie. "Cheer up, doll. I've got a running-spell somewhere. I'll rub it on your feet."

In a second she had taken a tiny box from her pocket, and had opened it. Inside was a green ointment. She rubbed it on the soles of Angela's feet.

"Oooh! You tickle!" said Angela,

83

screwing up her toes. "Don't!"

"Now get up, and see if you can walk," said the pixie. "Go on! Don't start ee-ing again, for goodness' sake. Walk after your little girl-mother before she has gone too far. You may even be able to run!"

Angela stood up. She wobbled a bit and sat down suddenly. She opened her mouth to squeak.

"No, don't start that noise again," said the pixie. "Up you get – that's right. Now quickly – off you go!"

And, to Angela's enormous surprise and delight, off she went! She was a

little unsteady at first, but she soon got along all right. It was fun. Her little feet pattered up the hill and round the corner.

"Look at that!" said a countrywoman, going home to tea. "Whatever is it?"

"My word! Is that a tiny fairy?" cried a little boy, leaning over a gate.

"I must get some new glasses!" said old Farmer Straws, looking across the hedge at Angela. "I can see a girl running by, but she only looks as small as a doll to me! Most peculiar. My eyes want seeing to!"

Joanna was over the top of the hill now. She turned her pram round to

push it instead of pull it, and she saw that Angela was not there. She gave a scream.

"Angela's gone! She must have fallen out! Oh, Sarah, I shall have to go back and look for her."

"You can't. We shall be very late for tea if you do," said Sarah. "Your mother will be cross."

"But I *must* go back!" said Joanna, tears coming into her eyes. "Poor, poor Angela! She may be broken!"

Well, Joanna set off back again over the top of the hill, and no sooner had she got halfway down it than, lo and behold, there was Angela, scurrying to meet her as fast as ever she could! Joanna could hardly believe her eyes.

"Angela! You're running! You must be alive! ANGELA! Oh, you darling, you're running!"

She picked Angela up and put her into the pram again. She tucked her up well, and then hurried after Sarah to tell her the great news.

"Sarah! I've got Angela. You'll hardly

believe it, but she was running up the hill!"

"I don't believe it," said Sarah at once.

"But it's true, Sarah. And I can prove it to you," said Joanna. "Look! She took off the pram-covers and turned up Angela's feet to show the bottoms of them to Sarah. They were quite dirty!

"There you are!" said Joanna. "The darling hadn't even shoes or stockings on, but it made no difference. She ran after me in her bare feet and got them all dirty. Isn't she a marvellous doll, Sarah?"

"Well, I'll believe it when I see her doing it," said Sarah.

"Oh, she'll do it again. You'll see!" said Joanna happily. "Darling Angela! When I get her home I shall wash her dirty little feet and make them clean again."

So she did. Angela enjoyed all the fuss and liked feeling her feet in the warm soapy water. But, oh dear, it really was a pity that Joanna had washed her feet, because, you see, she washed off the running-spell, of course. Now Angela would not be able to run again.

"There!" said Joanna, when she had finished. "Now your dirty little feet are clean again. Oh Angela – I can hardly believe you ran after me today – but you really, really did!"

88

She put Angela back into her pram and tucked her in. How sad she would have felt if she had known that the running-spell was all washed away!

Sarah never saw Angela running, and she doesn't believe it to this day – and even Joanna doesn't know whether she dreamt it or not! I would have loved to see Angela running by herself, wouldn't you?

89

The Black Sheep

You wouldn't believe how many toys there were in Gemma's nursery! Teddy bears, dolls, dogs, elephants, a rocking-horse, two cats, three rabbits, and a mouse, to say nothing of trains, cars and books!

Gemma had a great many uncles and aunts, and they all spoilt her and brought her toys every week, so that really it was quite difficult for her to find room for all of them.

And then one day Uncle Jack brought her a black sheep. It was a large sheep, not big enough for Gemma to ride on, but big enough for her to sit her dolls on. She played with it a lot, and squeezed it to make it say "Baa, baa!" all day long.

The other toys were not sure that they liked the black sheep.

"It's no cousin of *mine*," said the snow-white woolly lamb. "All my family are as white as I am."

"I'm tired of its voice," said the ragdoll.

"I thought sheep were white," said the pink cat.

"And I thought cats were black, brown, tabby, or ginger!" snapped the black sheep suddenly. "I've never seen a *pink* cat before. Pink indeed!"

Now the pink cat was one of the oldest toys in the nursery, and very easily offended. She swished her short tail angrily, and tried hard to think of

91

something rude to say. But all she could think of was, "Baa, baa, black sheep". So she said it, and laughed as she said it.

The toys thought this was funny. They laughed. They made a ring round the surprised sheep and sang. "Baa, baa, black sheep, have you any wool?"

"Don't be silly," said the black sheep.

"Go on, answer us," said the pink cat. "You've got to say you have three bags full."

"I haven't," said the sheep. "I'm not the sheep in the nursery rhyme, silly. Be quiet!"

But the toys wouldn't be quiet. Every time they saw the sheep they asked him the same silly question, "Baa, baa, black sheep, have you any wool?"

The black sheep never answered, but he grew sad. He was quite a nice creature really, and he didn't mind being black. He was a kindly animal, but the toys didn't give him any chance to show his kindness. They just teased him.

One day Gemma took him down the garden with her. A workman was whitewashing the henhouse, and Gemma went to watch him. She put the sheep on a box nearby and stood watching the slish-slosh of the workman's brush. It was a lovely sight. Gemma wished she could whitewash the wall too. She thought she would go and ask Mother if she might have a brush and help the workman. So off she went.

Now after a few minutes the workman stepped back to see how his work looked – and he knocked against the black sheep. The sheep fell off the box straight into the bucket of whitewash!

He *was* surprised. He went under the whitewash and then bobbed up again. The workman didn't see him until he bent to dip his brush into the pail again.

94

"Goodness me! What's this?" he said, and he picked the sheep out of the whitewash. The black sheep was now as white as snow!

"It's one of the little girl's toys," he said in surprise. "Well, well! It had better dry in the sun. I'll give it to Gemma when she comes back."

So he stood it in the sun to dry. Gemma didn't come back, because Mother had told her she must get ready for her walk. So the workman handed the sheep to the home help and asked her to put it in Gemma's room.

The sheep had dried snowy white. He looked most beautiful. He was still very surprised, and could hardly believe it was himself.

The toys were astonished to see a snowy-white sheep. They didn't know him at all. They looked at him and greeted him politely.

"Good afternoon. What a fine fellow you are! We are pleased to see you in our nursery."

"Good afternoon," said the sheep,

most astonished. It was funny to think that the toys didn't know him.

"Have you come to live with us?" asked the lamb.

"Yes," said the sheep.

"Perhaps you have come instead of the horrid black sheep that used to live here," said one of the dolls. "He was so ugly."

"And so rude," said the pink cat.

"If he comes back you must fight him," said the ragdoll.

96

"Why was he so horrid?" asked the sheep, most surprised to hear all these things about himself. "Perhaps he was quite nice really, and you didn't give him a chance."

"Oh no, he was just as horrid as you are nice," said the black dog. "Will you join our games when we play tonight?"

"Yes, thank you," said the sheep. The toys had never asked him to join in their games before.

Well, the sheep had a fine time. Everyone was as nice as could be to him. So he was nice back to them, and the toys thought he was a fine fellow.

"We do hope that horrid black sheep will never come back again," said the pink cat to the sheep. "We really do. If only he had been as nice as you, he would have been all right – but he was a rude fellow."

The sheep said nothing; but then, whatever do you think happened?

Gemma found the sheep in the toy cupboard and took him out with great surprise.

"Why!" she cried. "Are you a new toy? No – you're not! You're just my dear old black sheep covered in whitewash! Alice told me you had fallen into the bucket. Well, I'll soon get you right again."

She took a stiff brush and she brushed the sheep. How she brushed him! The whitewash flew off him in clouds of dust. He became grey – he became black – and at last there he stood, as black as before, with a little pile of dry whitewash dust beside him.

The toys stared in surprise. They didn't know what to think or say. And then the ragdoll spoke.

"Black sheep, so it was really you all the time! We didn't know – we thought you were somebody new and nice."

"Well," said the black sheep, "I'm not somebody new – but I hope I'm nice. Surely if I am nice when I am white, I must be nice when I am black? I'm just the same inside."

"So you are, so you are," said the ragdoll. "I feel ashamed of myself for having been horrid before. We'll be friends now, Black Sheep – and we'll never, never ask you again if you've any wool."

So now they all live happily together in Gemma's playroom. Wasn't it a good thing the sheep fell into the pail of whitewash?

It Serves You Right, Jumbo!

Up on the mantelpiece of the children's playroom were six china figures and a little green clock. The toys often looked up at them at night when they came alive, and wished the china ornaments could come down and play with them. But the mantelpiece was too high up, and they couldn't.

There was a china rabbit there with cock-up ears. There were two little horses with long tails. There was a small frisky lamb, and there was a pretty shepherdess to look after him.

And last of all there was a big grey china elephant. He had a long trunk in the front and a little tail behind.

At night all the china figures came alive at exactly the same moment as the toys did, and then you should have seen the high jinks that went on up on the mantelpiece! The lamb frisked away from the pretty shepherdess, and she ran after him, afraid that he would fall off. The horses galloped after one another and chased each other round and round the clock. The rabbit went to a tiny hole at the back of the mantelpiece and tried to burrow down it. He did so want a burrow of his own.

The elephant was more tiresome. He was bigger than the others, and they didn't much like playing with him because he was clumsy and nearly knocked them off the high mantelpiece.

And his trunk was most annoying. He had discovered that he could use it like a hand – and he did!

He pulled the tail of the frisky lamb. He chased the shepherdess and pulled her hair down. He lay in wait for the two horses and caught hold of their flying manes with his trunk as they passed.

"Don't!" they said, trying to shake free. "You spoil our game. Don't!"

As for the little rabbit, Jumbo gave him the fright of his life. He took hold of him with his trunk and set him high up on his back, and then walked up and down the mantelpiece with the poor bunny holding on for all he was worth, trembling with fear.

102

"Don't! Let me down! Please let me down!" begged the little rabbit. "I'm frightened. I don't like it."

"Well, you ought to," said the elephant. "Why, at the Zoo out in the Big World there are elephants a thousand times bigger than I am – and children *pay* to have rides on their backs! And I'm giving you a ride for nothing. I'm very kind."

"You're not," called the lamb, hiding behind the clock. "You're horrid! You're always chasing us and teasing us with that nasty trunk of yours. You let poor Rabbit down. He will fall off with fright if you don't!"

Instead of that the elephant began to try and gallop up and down the mantelpiece – and then a dreadful thing happened! The horses came unexpectedly round the clock and bumped into him. He slipped and fell. The rabbit slid off his back and landed unhurt on the mantelpiece – but, oh dear, the elephant fell right over the edge!

CRASH!

After that dreadful sound there was a silence.

The toys down below were horrified. The horses, lamb, shepherdess and rabbit up on the mantelpiece were too frightened even to peep over and see what had happened to the elephant.

"He's broken," said the toy panda at last.

"Smashed to pieces," said the teddy-bear.

"That's the end of him," said the curly-haired doll. "And I should think it was probably his own fault. He was teasing the rabbit as usual."

The china figures peeped over the edge of the mantelpiece at last. They gazed down in silence at the pieces of the elephant in the fireplace.

"I want him mended," said the rabbit suddenly. "I do! He was horrid to me, but I can't bear to see him like that. Mend him, toys, please do!"

105

"Well! You *are* a forgiving little creature," said the panda in surprise. "But if you really do want him mended, we'll get some glue and stick the pieces together." So they got a tube of glue and began to stick together the pieces of the broken china elephant. There were fourteen of them, so it was a bit of a jigsaw to put them together.

"Here's an ear," said the panda.

"Here's a leg," said the teddy-bear.

"And here's a bit of his tummy," said the curly-haired doll.

Well, the toys worked hard with the glue and at last they had mended poor old Jumbo. Every piece was stuck in its place again, and there he stood, looking a bit cracked here and there, but still an elephant.

But wait a bit – there was something funny about him! The toys looked and looked – and then the teddy-bear gave a squeal of laughter.

"Oh, look! Golly, you've stuck his tail on the front of him, where his trunk ought to be – and you've stuck his

trunk at the back, instead of his tail!"

Well, well, well, so they had! No wonder old Jumbo looked strange. He was really very upset about it.

"Oh, my, whatever shall I do?" he said. "I can't pick up things with my tail, you know – and if my trunk is at the back of me I shan't be able to see what to pick up with that!"

"Well, seeing that you used your

trunk for teasing people, pulling their hair and manes and their tails, Jumbo, it's just as well I made that mistake," giggled the panda. "You do look funny! Anyway, you can't tease anyone now."

"Did you do it on purpose?" said the teddy-bear, looking at the panda suddenly.

"I might have. You never know," said the panda. "Anyway, there's no reason why I shouldn't be a bit of a tease, too, is there?"

There was nothing to be done about it. The elephant had a tail for a trunk and a trunk for a tail, and there he stood on the carpet, waiting for somebody to come along in the morning and pick him up.

The children's mother found him there and put him back on the mantelpiece without even noticing he looked different. Jumbo felt very much ashamed of his appearance. He went to hide behind the clock.

The little rabbit was there. "I'm sorry for you," he said timidly. "I'm glad you can't lift me on to your back and frighten me again – but I am very sorry you fell off the mantelpiece and got broken."

Wasn't that nice of him? Jumbo felt sorry too that he had teased the rabbit, and he hung his head down and swished the tail that now grew from it.

"Let's be friends," said the rabbit. "The lamb has his shepherdess and the horses have each other. We haven't anyone."

So now they are friends, which is nice for them both. But I do wish you could see how funny poor old Jumbo looks with his trunk at the back and his tail at the front!

The Naughty
Sailor Doll

Sailor Doll is so *tiresome*," said the golden-haired doll. "He does such silly things."

"Yes. He tied the clockwork mouse's tail to a bootlace yesterday when he was asleep," said the teddy-bear. "And when the mouse woke up Sailor told him a snake was eating his tail up, and he ran for miles round the nursery, with his bootlace tail behind him. He really did think it was a snake."

"And Sailor wetted me through," said the black toy dog. "He got the little watering-can and filled it. Then he climbed up on the table and watered me when I sat underneath. I thought it was raining."

"And he burst a paper bag near me

and told me the captain of the soldiers had shot at me," said the clown. "I felt awfully frightened. I thought I was wounded and I looked all over myself to see."

"And now he's discovered that money-box up on the shelf," said the teddy-bear. "It's just like a letter-box – you know, it's got a slit to put pennies in – and Sailor keeps posting things in it."

"He's posted my best handkerchief," said Angela, the doll.

"And he tried to post my best brooch yesterday. I just stopped him in time," said the baby doll.

"He'll post the clockwork mouse's key if he's not careful," said the clown. The mouse gave a squeal of terror.

"It's all right. If Sailor does that we'll punish him," said the golden-haired doll in a loud voice.

Sailor didn't care! If he was in a naughty mood he'd do anything. Why, he had once climbed up to the wash-basin, put in the plug, and turned on a tap! The toys were very frightened when the water overflowed all over the carpet.

"Get into the ark, get into Noah's ark, there are floods coming!" the naughty sailor doll had shouted.

So you see, he really would do anything, and when he heard the toys talking about him he felt naughtier than ever.

He took one of the baby doll's shoes and posted that in the money-box. He took the little necklace belonging to Angela, broke it, and posted the beads one by one, Clinkity-clinkity-clink they went, and dropped down among the coins in the box.

He even took the tiny plates out of the dolls' house and posted those in the

112

money-box, too. The dolls were very angry indeed.

"That's too bad of you, Sailor!" they cried. "Now we can't give our party. You've posted the plates."

"What do I care?" said Sailor "You wouldn't have asked me to your party, anyhow. I don't mind that, though – I go to plenty of parties!"

That was quite true. He had a little goblin friend who lived in the garden outside and often asked him to parties. Sailor always looked smart in his blue trousers, blue sailor-vest with its white-bordered collar, little round hat, black shoes and a whistle on a white thread round his neck.

He loved parties and dancing. He was always going to them and having a good time. "Goodbye!" he would say. "I'm off again! See you at dawn!"

Sailor wondered what he could post next. The clockwork mouse's key, of course – and the railway train's key, too – and what about the key that wound up the little motor-car? He would pop each one through the slit in the red money-box – and *how* angry the toys would be!

So he took them all and ran to the money-box. The toys ran after him as soon as they saw what he had got. But down went the three keys into the box, and there they stayed, because the box couldn't be opened unless John, whose box it was, got the key from Mother and unlocked it to take out some of his money. And that might not be for three or four weeks!

"You are wicked, Sailor Doll!" cried Teddy.

"Yes, you really are," cried Clown. "Now we can't ride in the train or the car – and the mouse can't run across the floor."

"I don't care," said the sailor doll, and he didn't. "I'm going to a party tonight. And I shall want a bath before I go, dolls' house dolls. Get it ready for me!"

"Oh *dear* – that means you'll slop water all over the bathroom floor," said Teeny, the chief dolls' house doll. "And you always put the mats crooked. You're too big to come into our house."

"I'm coming, all the same," said Sailor, and, sure enough, he squeezed in

at the little door that night, squashed his way up the little stairs, and went into the bathroom. Teeny had got the bath ready.

A lot of whispering went on outside the bathroom door. It was one of the dolls giving a message from Clown to Teeny.

"He says you're to tell Sailor to put his clothes outside the door so that we can give them a good brushing before he goes to the party," whispered the little doll.

"But why *should* we brush his clothes?" whispered back Teeny fiercely. "Horrid creature he is! I don't want to brush his clothes!"

"Clown says you're to throw his clothes out of the window and he'll deal with them himself," whispered the tiny doll.

"What's all the whispering about?" shouted Sailor from the bathroom.

"Sailor, throw your things outside the door for brushing," called Teeny.

"Good idea," said Sailor, and out

came his blue sailor-vest with its white-bordered collar, his round hat, his blue trousers and his black shoes.

Teeny threw them out of the window to the panda, who was waiting down below. And what *do* you think he did? He didn't brush those clothes. Oh no! He and the other toys took them solemnly to the shelf where the money-box stood, and one by one they posted Sailor's clothes.

"There goes his hat!" said Clown, and posted it.

"There goes his sailor-vest," said Teddy, and posted it.

"There go his shoes," said Angela, and posted them.

"And there go his trousers," said the golden-haired doll, and posted those, too!

Sailor had his bath. He got out of it and dried himself. He put on his vest. Then he yelled for his clothes.

Nobody brought them. He yelled again.

"You can't have them, Sailor," called

118

Teeny. "They're all posted in the money-box."

"What!" shouted Sailor, hardly believing his ears. "Say that again."

"THEY'RE ALL POSTED IN THE MONEY-BOX!" shouted the toys together and the clockwork mouse gave a squeal of laughter.

Well! Sailor simply didn't know *what* to think. His clothes posted! What was he to wear, then? How could he go to a party without his clothes? He couldn't. Nobody would allow him to go in an undervest. And, anyway, he had terribly skinny legs. He didn't want anyone to see those.

He yelled loudly, "I don't believe you. Bring my clothes at once!"

A comic-looking head looked in at the window of the bathroom and made Sailor jump. It was Clown, grinning all over his face.

"Sorry, Sailor. But they really *are* posted. I mean, you love to post *our* things, and we thought it would be great fun to post *yours*. I say, what

skinny legs you've got!"

Sailor gave a howl of anger and misery. He believed Clown. He knew his clothes *had* been posted. The toys had done exactly the same to him as he had so often done to them.

And he didn't like it. He didn't like it one little bit. "I can't go to the party," he wailed. "I can't go out of the dolls'-house. I can't leave this bathroom. I've only got my vest. Clown, do lend me some clothes."

"Not I," said the clown. "You can come out in your vest if you like. We shan't mind. We shall love to see your

121

skinny legs. I never knew they were so spindly before. I wish the others could see them."

"Don't! Don't!" groaned Sailor, and he draped the little towel round his legs. "Oh, I'm so miserable."

"You're only feeling what you made *us* feel," said Clown. "Well, you'll get your clothes back when we get *our* things back – when the money-box is opened. And I can't *imagine* what John will say when he sees all the things inside."

I can't either! As for Sailor, he hasn't been to a party for three whole weeks, he hasn't been out of the dolls' house for days, and he spends all his time in the bathroom. He *is* so ashamed of his skinny legs!

Poor Sailor. He'll behave differently when he's got his clothes again, I'm sure.

He'd Better Be Careful!

One day Susan had a friend called Janie to tea. She wasn't very old, not quite five – and, dear me, how very, very spoilt she was!

Susan didn't like her at all, because whenever anything went wrong Janie screamed. How she screamed! It was a dreadful noise, and it made Janie's mother run to her at once and pick her up in alarm.

"What's the matter with you, darling?" she said. But Janie only screamed louder still.

"Did you hurt her?" asked Susan's mother, in surprise.

Susan shook her head. "No, Mummy. All that happened was Janie's brick castle fell over. So she screamed

because she was cross."

Janie screamed when her foot caught in the rug and she tripped over. She screamed when it was time to go home.

"You'll scream your head off one day," said Susan, solemnly. "I hope I'm there to see it!"

Now, when Janie had gone home, and Susan had gone to bed, and the playroom was quiet and empty, the toys came out to play.

"What a dreadful screamer that girl was!" said the ragdoll. "She made me jump so much that I nearly fell off my shelf."

"Horrible spoilt child," said the teddy bear. "I'd rather have our Susan any day."

The little nodding man didn't say anything. He couldn't help thinking that screaming was a very good idea if people were silly enough to let you have your own way when you screamed. He thought he would try it one day. He nodded his funny little head up and down, and thought what fun it would be to scream and scream so that all the toys came rushing to him and fussed over him, and let him do exactly what he wanted.

But he couldn't scream whilst Susan or her family were about, of course. He had to wait till they went away for their holiday. And then he began.

It started when the toys were running races round the playroom. There was a big crumb of chocolate

cake for a prize, and the nodding man wanted that very badly.

Just as the race began, he screamed. He stopped running and screamed very loudly indeed, so loudly that he startled even himself.

All the toys stopped running at once and crowded round him anxiously.

"What's the matter?" asked the ragdoll. "Why are you making that noise?"

"Are you hurt?" said the bear.

"Somebody t-t-trod on my foot," said the nodding man.

"Fibber!" said the cat. "Nobody was near you."

The nodding man screamed again and made the toys jump dreadfully.

"*Now* what's the matter?" said the ragdoll.

"The cat called me a fibber," said the nodding man, fiercely.

"But you've often been called a fibber and a storyteller, because you *are*," said the bear, "and you've never screamed about it before. Don't be silly, nodding man."

The nodding man at once screamed again, and the toys put their hands over their ears. "Isn't he dreadful when he screams?" said the ragdoll.

"Stop it, nodding man. If you really are hurt we will stop the race and you can nibble the chocolate crumb to make you better."

Well! That was exactly what the nodding man wanted, of course. How very, very nice! He didn't scream any more, but settled down on the lid of the brick-box and began to nibble the crumb of chocolate cake. He didn't offer even the clockwork mouse a bit.

It was a great pity that the toys gave in to him when he first screamed because after that he just kept on screaming whenever he wanted his own way. At first he got it, because the toys really were alarmed when he made such a noise. They thought that surely nobody would scream so loudly unless he was ill or hurt.

But after a while they got tired of letting him have his own way. "Why should we play hide and seek whenever *he* wants us to, instead of the games *we* want to play?" said the ragdoll.

"Why should we let him sleep in the doll's cot just because he screams to be allowed to?" said the big doll. "Either I have to sleep on the floor or we are so squashed up I can hardly move in the cot. Besides, sometimes his head nods when he is asleep and that's most annoying."

"He just screams to get his own way," said the clockwork mouse. "He knows we can't bear the noise, and so if we want him to stop we have to let him do what he wants. He's very naughty and very selfish."

"Then we won't take any more notice of him at all when he screams," said the ragdoll. "He saw that girl Janie doing it, I expect, and he's just copying her."

So the next time that the nodding man opened his mouth and screamed none of the toys took any notice at all. The ragdoll went on playing the musical box, turning the handle round and round, the bear went on dancing to it, the dolls sat and talked, and the cat and clockwork mouse went on building a house for themselves with the bricks.

The nodding man was very angry. What! Nobody came rushing to him to see what was the matter? Nobody asked him what he wanted? How horrid of everybody!

He screamed again, more loudly. Scream away, silly little man!

"I'll scream all day long!" said the nodding man, fiercely. "You won't like that."

"Don't be silly," said the teddy-bear,

and danced over to him and trod on his toe on purpose. It didn't really hurt the nodding man because the bear's paws were very soft. But he screamed as if an elephant had stamped on his foot.

Nobody took any notice. He took a deep breath. Aha! This time he would scream so hard that he would make them jump in fright!

So he screamed as loudly as he could, and his head nodded so much with the noise that the ragdoll looked at him in alarm. "You'll scream your head off if you go on like that, nodding man! You

131

will! I've often heard people warn children they will scream their heads off – and now I'm warning you!"

"Pooh!" said the nodding man. "And Pooh again! You can't frighten *me*! I don't believe you."

"Well, people don't usually give warnings unless there is some truth in them," said the ragdoll. "And I tell you, nodding man, if you go on like this you will most certainly scream your head off!"

The nodding man screamed again, angrily and loudly. He was so very annoyed at not having his own way. His head nodded up and down violently – and then, at his last loud scream, it jumped right off his shoulders and rolled across the floor!

That *did* make the toys take notice! They all jumped up at once in fright.

"He has screamed his head off," said the ragdoll in a scared whisper.

"We told him, we told him!" said the clockwork mouse, and burst into tears.

"What are we going to do about it?" said the bear staring at the nodding man's head on the floor. Then he looked at the nodding man's body. It seemed to be standing in great astonishment, and it turned itself round and round as if it was looking for something.

"Here I am!" squeaked the nodding man's head, and his little body walked over to it and picked it up. All the toys stared at the nodding man holding his head in his arms. Tears poured down the nodding man's face.

"I've done it," he whispered. "I've screamed my head off. I feel peculiar, toys. Put my head back again."

The ragdoll walked over to him. He took the nodding man's head and popped it on his shoulders again. But he had put it on the wrong way round, so when the nodding man wanted to walk forwards, he walked backwards, instead!

"Silly!" he cried. "You've put my head on back to front. Put it on right, or I'll scream."

"Now listen to me," said the ragdoll, sternly. "Your head can jolly well stay on back to front, if that's the way you are going to talk. Screaming indeed! Haven't you just lost your head, screamed it right off, through your bad temper? Let me tell you that you are

likely to scream it off again, if you behave like this – and *next* time *nobody* will put it on again for you. We shall put it inside the doll's teapot and put the lid on. How will you like that?"

Well, of course, the ragdoll would never have done a thing like that, but the nodding man really thought he might. So he spoke very humbly indeed:

"I'm sorry, ragdoll. Please put my head on the right way round. I shan't

scream again. It's a dreadful feeling to scream your head off."

"It must be," said the ragdoll. "Thank goodness I'm never likely to treat *my* head like that."

"Please put my head on right," begged the nodding man. "It's horrid to be back to front."

"I'll put your head right tomorrow,"

said the ragdoll. "It will do you good to feel peculiar for a little while. Now go away and let us forget about you and your screaming."

The nodding man felt cross and upset enough to scream for an hour, but he didn't. He walked backwards into a corner and sat down. His face was towards the toys, watching them at their play, but the rest of him was turned towards the wall. He felt funny and looked funny.

He had to stay like that till the next day, when Susan and her family coming home again. The ragdoll went to him and touched his head. It nodded just the same as ever. "I'll put it on the right way for you now," he said.

But he couldn't take the nodding man's head off! He just couldn't.

"Well, *now* what are we going to do?" he said.

"He'll have to scream his head off for the last time," said the clockwork mouse. "Then you can pick it up and put it on the right way round."

And will you believe it, that is exactly what the nodding man had to do! He screamed his loudest, his head flew off, and there it was on the floor. The ragdoll picked it up and put it on his shoulders the right way round.

"Oh! It does feel so nice to be the right way round," said the nodding man. "It really does. Thank you, ragdoll. I won't scream again."

"You'd better be careful!" said the teddy bear. "You know what will happen to your head if you *do* begin to scream again! It will pop off your shoulders – and into the teapot it will go!"

"It's a pity that girl Janie doesn't scream *her* head off!" said the ragdoll. "That would teach her a lesson! Perhaps she will one day."

"I hope I'm there," said the clockwork mouse with one of her giggles.

The Tiresome
Teddy Bear

Benny the bear was very tiresome. He hadn't got a tail and he wanted one. He kept on saying that he wanted one, and all the toys were tired of hearing him.

"I want a tail! Why shouldn't I have a tail? The toy monkey has one, and so has the horse. The pink cat has one, and so has the black dog. Even the clockwork mouse has a tail, and what he wants with such a nice long one I really don't know! It's wasted on him."

"It isn't," said the clockwork mouse, crossly.

"It is," said the bear.

"It *isn't*," said the mouse.

"It *is*," said Benny, loudly. The clockwork mouse ran off to a corner. All the toys knew that the bear would go

139

on saying "It is" for hours. He always did. So it was a wise thing to run away and say no more.

"Bears don't have tails," said the panda.

"They do," said Benny.

"They don't," said the panda.

"They DO!" said Benny. The panda ran off and turned his back on the bear. He was just impossible.

The teddy bear looked longingly at the toy monkey's tail. It was such a lovely long one. Why shouldn't the monkey spare half for him? He went up to Micky the monkey and spoke to him.

"Micky! You have such a long tail that it must get in your way sometimes, let me have half of it, you'd be glad to be without a long tail."

"I shouldn't," said Micky.

"You would," said Benny.

"I should not," said Micky.

"You WOULD!" said Benny. The monkey turned his back and said no more. And then Benny did a dreadful thing. He fetched a pair of scissors and

140

snipped off half of Micky's long tail!
The monkey gave such a yell that all
the toys hurried up at once.

"You wicked bear!" cried the panda.

"You bad teddy!" shouted the
monkey. Benny tried to stick the half-
tail behind him, but the toys pulled it
away. The big doll fetched a needle and
cotton and began to sew the snipped
tail together again. The monkey cried

bitterly. "It will never be the same again!" he wept. "Never! Never!"

Benny wasn't a bit sorry. He saw the clockwork mouse in the corner and went up to him. "You don't need your tail!" he said. "What does a mouse like you want with a tail? You don't hang yourself up by it as Micky the monkey does. You don't wag it like the dog does. Give it to me!"

He pulled hard at the little mouse-tail. It came off with a snap and the mouse gave a squeal.

"My tail's off! He pulled it off! Oh, oh, I do feel dreadful. I'm cold without my tail. He's pulled it off!"

Benny walked about the nursery holding the mouse-tail behind him, seeing how it looked. The toys ran and took it from him.

In the fight a bit of the tail was pulled off, and when the little clockwork mouse at last got it back again it was shorter than before. He was very sad.

"I shall look funny with such a short tail! I shall feel funny, too. Oh, you wicked bear!"

The toys looked angrily at Benny. This was getting very serious. Nobody's tail would be safe if Benny went on like this! The panda and the doll felt glad they had no tails to be pulled off. The black dog and the pink cat looked round at their own tails to make sure they were safe. The pink cat sat down hard on hers, and the black dog backed into the door of the doll's house, so that his tail was safely in the hall.

"I shall get a tail somehow," said the tiresome bear. "I shall, so there!"

"You will not!" said the panda, who was busy sticking the mouse's tail on again.

"I will!" said the bear.

"You will *not*!" said the panda

"I WILL!" said Benny, and everyone felt certain that he would. Tiresome people so often get their own way. It was very annoying.

The panda sat and thought hard. He

was very good at thinking, and out of his thoughts there came a little plan. He went to tell it to the others.

"We'd better *give* Benny a tail!" he said. "If we don't he'll steal one again, and make somebody unhappy. We'll *give* him one – and make him tired of it very quickly!"

"How?" asked the big doll.

"You'll see," said the panda. He went off to the string-box and pulled out quite a long bit of string. He took the

scissors and snipped it into three bits. Then he got the big doll to hold the bits for him whilst he knotted them at the top, and then plaited them neatly. He knotted them again at the bottom, so that the plait wouldn't come undone.

"There!" he said, "That will make a fine tail!" He called the bear to him.

"Look, Benny," he said, "here is a fine tail for you. It is nice and long and strong, and I daresay if you are good-tempered it will grow a fine wag in it. Shall I get the big doll to sew it on for you?"

"Oooh, yes!" said Benny, in delight. "My word, it's splendid, isn't it? Hurry, big doll, and sew it on."

The big doll did sew it on, very firmly indeed. The bear was terribly pleased with it. It hung down behind him exactly like a real tail, and he could even swing it a little from side to side.

"It's the finest tail in the nursery!" said the bear, boastfully.

"It isn't," said the monkey, and he hung himself upside down on his,

146

swinging from a chair-back very gracefully.

"It is," said the bear.

The monkey frowned and went to the panda. "Why do you give him a tail?" he asked. "It only makes him worse than ever."

"Wait till he's asleep," whispered the panda. So the toys waited. And, as soon as Benny was fast asleep, the panda did a very strange thing. He climbed up to the nursery cupboard, where mother

147

kept the nursery jam and honey and
sugar and biscuits – and he dipped the
spoon into the honey! He climbed down
carefully and went to the sleeping bear.
He dabbed honey on Benny's new tail –
all down it, sweet honey that smelt
wonderful. Then back he went with the
spoon.

Now, the next day, as Panda very well
knew, the children were going to take
their toys into the garden and give
them a picnic. That was what Panda
was waiting for! The toys were all taken
out in a bunch and set on the grass.
Then the children ran back to get the
tea-things.

148

"Get up and show the birds your tail, Benny," cried the panda. So the bear got up – but no sooner had he walked more than a few steps than the bees smelt the honey on his tail!

"Zzzzzzzz!" Down flew a honey-bee at once, and settled on Benny's tail! "Zzzoooom!" Down flew another – and another – and another. Benny squealed and ran away down the path. The bees flew after him, buzzing loudly.

"Go away, go away!" shouted Benny.

"ZZZZZoooom!" hummed the bees, and buzzed all round him. Soon there

were twenty or more, trying to settle on his tail to take the honey. Benny couldn't understand it, for he had no idea that the panda had dabbed his tail with honey. He ran here and there, squealing.

"They're after your tail, Benny, they're after your tail!" shouted the panda. "Sit down on it!"

So Benny sat down on his tail, but the bees buzzed round him all the more, trying to get at the honey.

He got up and ran away again, trying to hit the bees as they flew near. One stung him on the nose, and he began to sob.

"Oh, I'm stung! Oh, the bees are after me! Oh, Panda, Panda, cut off my tail, quickly! Please, please do! The bees will sting me to death."

He ran to the panda. But Panda shook his head. "No, Benny," he said. "You wanted a tail. You took the monkey's tail, and the mouse's, too. Now we've given you one of your own. You must keep it."

"I don't want a tail, I don't want a tail," wailed Benny. "Take it away. Oh, oh, there are two bees on it now. Quick, pull my tail off, Panda. PULL IT OFF!"

"NO!" said Panda. "You wanted a tail, you've got one, and you can keep it. Don't be tiresome!"

"You'd only want another tail if we took away the one you've got," said the big doll.

"I wouldn't," said the bear.

"You would," said the doll.

"I WOULDN'T," said Benny. The big doll said no more, but turned away. The bear ran after her, a score of bees buzzing round him.

"I'm sorry I talked like that, I'm sorry I took other people's tails, I'm sorry I'm such a tiresome bear!" he wept. "Take this tail away and give me another chance. I'll be better, I promise. I'll be better."

"Well, we'll see," said the big doll. She took hold of the bear's tail, and pulled at it hard, till all the stitches broke, and the tail came away. She threw it to the bees, who at once fastened on it, sipping the honey eagerly. The bear gave a yell, because it hurt him to have his tail pulled off like that. He rubbed himself, sat down and wept loudly.

"You're a baby," said the panda.

"I'm not," wept the bear.

"You ARE!" said the panda. And for once in a way the bear didn't answer back again. He sat and watched the bees on his old tail. It was all very strange. Bees didn't go after anyone else's tail. Why should they go after his? He saw the panda and the big doll laughing together, but they wouldn't tell him why.

"I suppose it's because I'm just a tiresome bear," thought Benny, sadly. "Well, I won't be tiresome any more. I won't! I won't!"

But you will, Benny, you will, you will!

The Doll
in the Cushion

In Jeanie's nursery was a little rubber
doll that squeaked whenever she was
pressed. "Eeeee!" she went like a
mouse, and Jeanie laughed and thought
she was a funny little doll.

"I shall call you Squealie," she said,
"because you squeal and squeak."

Squealie lived in the toy-cupboard
with two toy clowns, three teddies, two
more dolls, the bricks, the train, and
some soft animals. She would have
been very happy indeed if only the toys
wouldn't have made her squeak so
much! She was very small, and anybody
was strong enough to squeeze her and
make her squeak.

Even the clockwork mouse could
squeeze the little rubber doll, and

whenever the pink teddy bear wound him up at night, the very first thing the mouse did was to rush after poor Squealie, squash her very tightly and make her cry, "Eeee! Eeee! Eeee!"

"Please don't," Squealie would say. "Please don't. You squash all my breath out of me and I don't like it. It's not kind of you. I'm only meant to be squeezed by children. After all, I can *talk* to you – I don't want to keep squeaking to you."

But the toys still went on squeezing poor Squealie. She hadn't any clothes on except rubber ones, and she didn't like her tummy squashed so hard.

"Eeee! Eeee! Eeee!" she cried all night long.

Now, one night she couldn't bear it any longer, so she looked for a place to hide. She thought the brick-box would be a good place. She crept inside and hid between the bricks and the box. But the clockwork mouse had seen her creeping inside and he ran to the box, lifted up the lid, and jumped in. "Eeee! Eeee! Eeee!" cried Squealie, as the mouse squeezed her to make her squeal.

She began to cry. She ran away – and wherever do you suppose she hid next? She was small enough to climb inside the teapot belonging to the big toy-teaset! It was quite a big teapot and Squealie could just squeeze inside. She settled the lid over her head and crouched there, looking out through the spout at all the toys.

"Where's Squealie?" cried the pink Teddy, looking all round. "I want to squeeze her."

"She went into the teapot,"

whispered the red-haired doll, with a giggle.

"Into the *teapot*!" said the teddy in surprise. "Does she think she's a tea-leaf or something?"

"We'll go and ask her!" cried the big clown, and all the toys ran to the teapot. The clockwork mouse peeped down the spout and shouted loudly:

"Hi! Are you a tea-leaf? Will you pour out?"

"Let's try and see!" giggled the big clown, and he tipped up the teapot. Of course the rubber doll was too big to

157

pour out of the spout, but she got such a shock that she squeaked loudly, "Eeee Eeee!"

The small clown took off the lid. The rubber doll climbed out and ran away again. Oh dear, why couldn't the toys leave her alone for a little while! The toys were all going after her when the red-haired doll gave a yell. She had fallen into the domino-box, and the toys had to stop and get her out. When they turned round to see where Squealie had gone to, they couldn't see her. She was gone!

Where do you suppose she was? She was in a very good hiding-place this

time. There was a cushion on the nursery chair, and one side of it had come undone a little. The rubber doll saw the undone part, and she climbed through it into the cushion! She lay down in the dark softness of the cushion, and hoped nobody would find her.

Nobody did! Nobody thought of looking inside a cushion, and so Squealie lay there quite safely all night long, and nobody squeezed her at all to make her squeak. She was very glad.

Now next day Jeanie came into the nursery to have her breakfast. Mother came too, and she sat down heavily on the cushion inside which Squealie was hiding.

159

Well, of course, Mother's heavy body squeezed poor Squealie so much that she was squashed quite flat. She squeaked at once. "Eeee! Eeee! Eeee!"

"Goodness gracious! I've sat on the cat!" cried Mother, and she sprang up at once. But there was no cat there, only the cushion. Mother was surprised. "I really thought I heard the cat squealing," she said. She sat down again – and Squealie squeaked loudly, "EeeeeeeeeeeeeeEEEE!"

Up got Mother again in a hurry. She took the cushion up and looked

underneath it. There was nothing there. She simply couldn't understand it.

"I shan't sit on this chair any more," she said. "I don't like the noise it makes." So she took another chair and sat down without any noise at all.

Now the toys had been peeping through the door of the toy-cupboard all this time, and when they saw and heard what was happening, they laughed and laughed and laughed. They knew quite well that Squealie must be hiding inside the cushion and that Mother had sat on her.

Well, the next thing that happened was that Jeanie sat down on the cushion to dress the red-haired doll.

"EeeeeeEE!" squeaked poor Squealie inside, almost squashed flat.

"Goodness!" cried Jeanie in surprise, and she jumped up at once. "Have *I* sat on the cat?"

But no, she hadn't. It was all very mysterious and Jeanie couldn't *imagine* where the noise came from. She sat

161

down on the chair again, and once more the squealing noise came.

"It sounds like Squealie under the cushion," said Jeanie, and she lifted up the cushion to see. But of course Squealie was *inside*, not underneath.

Then it was time for Jeanie to go out, so she had to go and put on her coat and hat. Whilst she was in the bedroom the cat came into the nursery. He jumped up on the cushion at once. "EEEEEEEEEEE!" squeaked Squealie.

The cat jumped down in fright. The toys in the toy-cupboard laughed so much that they couldn't stand up! The red-haired doll who was on the floor nearby laughed till the tears ran down her red cheeks. The cat licked them up, and thought about the strange cushion.

But before he could make up his mind about it, Gran came into the room with Jeanie. "Just let me see if this button wants sewing on your coat," she said, and sat down on the cushion.

"EEEEEeeeeEEEEeeee!" squealed the rubber doll, for Gran was big and heavy. Gran jumped up at once in

astonishment. The toys laughed till they made a noise and the cat ran to the toy-cupboard to see what the fuss was about.

"Did you hear that cushion make a noise, Jeanie?" asked Gran, shaking the cushion.

"Yes, it *keeps* making noises," said Jeanie. "It sounds like my rubber doll, Squealie."

"Most extraordinary," said Gran. She pressed the cushion all over – and suddenly she felt the little rubber body of Squealie inside! "Why, there's something in the cushion!" she cried.

She undid the cushion cover a little more and then slipped her hand in. She pulled out poor Squealie.

"Why, here's your rubber doll!" she said. "Did *you* hide her there, Jeanie?"

"No, I didn't, Gran," said Jeanie, most surprised. "She must have crept there herself."

"Of course she didn't!" said Gran. "What would she want to hide away for?"

Squealie was put back into the toy-cupboard, and the hole in the end of the cushion was sewn up. Squealie was glad to be out of the cushion, for it was really dreadful to be sat on so often.

The toys could hardly speak to her for laughing. Squealie looked at them.

"It may have been funny to *you*," she said, "it was simply dreadful for *me*! Still, I'm glad you had a good laugh – but please, as I've given you such a nice lot of giggling, won't you be kind to me and not squeeze me any more? I really am afraid my squeak is wearing out now."

"All right, Squealie, we won't squeeze you any more," promised the big clown. "I've never laughed so much in my life! Oh dear – I'm going to laugh again!"

And he did. He made such a noise that the cat came along again and peeped into the cupboard. "What's the joke?" he asked.

But nobody told him. They were afraid he might squeeze Squealie if they told him about her, and toys don't like a cat's sharp claws!

Tig,
the Brownie Robber

There was once a robber brownie called Tig. He was big and fat and vain, and had twenty servant brownies who followed him everywhere. Tig was a rogue. He and his twenty little servants would creep up to a village in the night, surround it, and then, with loud shouts and yells, frighten all the people so that they came rushing out of their homes. Then the brownies would run into the open doors and steal anything they could lay their hands on.

Everybody was afraid of them.

One of the servants always carried a large trunk, full of Tig's beautiful coats. Tig wore all kinds of colours, and his coats were sewn with silver and gold, and set with precious stones. He was very proud of them indeed.

Now one day, as Tig and his servants passed quietly through a wood on their way to a village they meant to surprise that night, they were seen by a small pixie whose name was Shrimpy, because he was so little. He heard the sound of quiet tramping, and looked out of the hole in the tree in which he was living. How excited he was to see the robbers!

"If anyone catches those robbers they'll get a sack of gold!" thought Shrimpy with joy. "Now, I am a clever pixie. Maybe if I follow the robbers I shall learn their ways and find some way of catching them all!"

So he jumped out of his tree and

began to follow the robbers. But he hadn't gone very far, creeping behind trees and watching them, before Tig caught sight of him. Tig had very sharp eyes in his round fat face, and they didn't miss anything.

"Oho!" he said in a large voice. "Catch that pixie, servants. He is following us!"

And in a second Shrimpy was caught and taken before the robber chief.

"What shall we do with him?" said one of the servants. "Shall we throw him into the lake?"

"Or tie him to the topmost branch of a tree?" said another.

Shrimpy didn't like the sound of this at all. "Please let me join your band," he said, thinking that he could easily escape at any time. "I will do any work you like."

"Ho, ho!" laughed Tig. "What! A shrimp like you do work for us! What work could *you* do?"

"I am very strong," said Shrimpy.

"Well, if he's so strong, let him carry your trunk of coats, Master!" said the brownie whose job it was to carry the trunk on his shoulder all day. He was getting very tired of it.

"Very well," said Tig, with a big grin all over his fat face. "You shall join our band, and carry my trunk, Shrimpy."

So poor Shrimpy had to put the heavy trunk on his small shoulder and carry it about all that day. Dear me, it *was* heavy! He didn't like it at all, and he wished he hadn't tried to interfere with the robbers.

"Never mind," thought Shrimpy, his

quick little brain working hard. "Maybe I can find some way to catch the robbers yet. Oh, if only I could!"

It was cold weather. In the daytime the brownies were warm, but at night they shivered and shook. Tig was all right because he just put on a few of his extra coats, and was as warm as toast. But the servants had no extra coats, and they felt very cold indeed.

That night was really freezing. Tig gave orders that his servants were to camp under the trees, and he would march on a little way ahead to a cottage he knew. A friend of his lived there, and he meant to have supper with him.

"I'll be back in the morning," he told his men. "Shrimpy, you come with me. I may want to change my coat tonight, when I see my friend, so you must carry my trunk. And if there is any message to give my men, you shall go back with it."

Shrimpy groaned. Oh dear! He had so hoped that he could find a hole in a tree and sleep there, warm and comfortable that night. Now he had to carry that horrid trunk through the wood for miles!

He put it on his shoulder and followed Tig. How glad he was when the master brownie came to the cottage and was welcomed by his friend!

"I shan't want any of my coats after all," said Tig, with a grin. "I knew I shouldn't. But I thought it would do you good to carry that trunk a bit longer!"

And with that the unkind brownie slammed the door and left Shrimpy outside with the trunk.

"All that way to go back with this hateful trunk!" groaned poor Shrimpy. "Oh, it's too bad! I could have been resting all this long time. How I hate Tig!"

He put the trunk on his shoulder and staggered back through the wood with it, thinking how horrid Tig was, and how he wished he could punish him. And slowly a plan came into his quick little mind.

He was so pleased with it that he almost danced for joy, though the trunk felt heavier than ever. At last he got back to the camp. He called to the men.

"There is a message from the master!"

"What is it?" cried the men, gathering round him, shivering, for their fire did not give out much heat.

"You are to warm yourselves by digging a big pit tonight," said Shrimpy. "It is to be a trap for an enemy, and must be finished quickly, before the daylight comes. If it is finished well, Tig says you may each have a coat of his to keep you warm tonight. I will button them round you. Now, work hard!"

Grumbling loudly the tired servants took spades from their bags and began to dig a big pit. When it was finished they were certainly very warm. Shrimpy was busy whilst they were digging. He was unpacking the trunk.

Inside there were a great many coats, all made very large indeed to fit Tig, who really was an enormous brownie. Shrimpy got each one out, and felt his way to young trees that stood here and there in the wood. He carefully put a coat round each slender tree, but did not button it up.

"Is the pit finished?" he asked at last. "Good! Now, I have taken the coats out and got them ready for you to put on. You had better put them on back to front and then the cold wind will not blow down your chests. You can have your backs against a tree."

He took the first brownie and led him to a tree round which he had put one of Tig's big coats. He made the servant slip his arms into the sleeves back to front – and then, very quickly, Shrimpy buttoned the coat up tightly down the back – round the tree-trunk! And there was the servant buttoned to the tree so that he couldn't possibly get away, for he could not reach to undo the buttons!

One by one Shrimpy buttoned up the tired brownies. It was dark, so they did not see what Shrimpy was doing. One or two of them grumbled because the tree felt so hard and uncomfortable at their back – but they were so very tired that they fell asleep even though they were so uncomfortable.

Shrimpy was simply delighted. He had fastened all the servants to the trees! They couldn't undo the coats! They could only yell for help – and that was just what he wanted them to do! Aha! Wait for the morning, Tig, and see what happens to you!

As soon as daylight came creeping through the trees, little Shrimpy ran to the pit that the servants had dug the night before. It was very deep, and the sides were very straight. Shrimpy gathered armfuls of bracken and pulled sticks and twigs from the bushes. He strewed them over the pit opening so that it could not be seen.

Then he hid himself in a hole of a tree and waited to see what would happen.

As soon as the servants awoke they tried to free themselves from the trees they were buttoned to – but they could not. They struggled and shouted, they tried to reach the buttons at the back of the tree, but it was no use at all. The coats were strong and big, and held them prisoner.

Shrimpy looked out of his tree and giggled. The servants saw him and shouted at him angrily:

"Come and set us free! Come and unbutton us!"

But Shrimpy laughed and shook his head.

"You wait till Tig comes!" roared the angry brownies. "He will untie us, and catch you and punish you! This is a very silly trick to play!"

Just then Shrimpy heard Tig coming along, singing loudly.

"Here comes robber brownie Tig.
Fat and plump and round and big!" sang Tig, very pleased after his good warm night and fine hot breakfast.

"Master! Master! Help us!" yelled his servants. "Shrimpy has buttoned us to the trees in your coats and we can't get away!"

Tig stopped singing and glared through the trees. He could just see his servants there, neatly buttoned up to the trunks! He gave a roar and rushed towards them.

Shrimpy appeared round the trunk of a tree and grinned at him. "You wicked little thing!" cried Tig, and tore after Shrimpy. Shrimpy ran to where the pit was hidden beneath bracken and twigs.

He leapt lightly over it, but Tig did not know the pit was there, and he fell heavily into it – plonk!

He roared again and got up. But the pit was so deep and steep that he couldn't get out! There he was, caught in the hole his servants had dug – and there were his servants, crying and howling because their master had disappeared into the pit and couldn't rescue them!

Shrimpy laughed with joy, and then

set off to the nearest town. Very soon he was back with fifty pixies, fairies and elves. How they laughed to see the twenty brownies buttoned up in big coats to tree-trunks, and Tig stamping round the deep pit, trying in vain to get out!

"You are the cleverest little pixie in the world!" they said to Shrimpy. "You shall have a sack of gold for your clever night's work!"

He did – and with it he bought himself a large toadstool, with three windows in the top and a door in the stem, cobweb curtains, and some lovely furniture.

"I shan't have to live in a hole in a tree any more!" he said joyfully. "I am very grand now. I shall get a wife as small as myself, and we will live in our toadstool house together and have a fine time!"

As for Tig and the brownies, they were sent off to the moon for one hundred years, so they won't worry anyone for a long, long time!

Billy's
Little Boats

Once upon a time, not so very long ago, a crowd of little brownies had to leave their home hurriedly. They lived in Bluebell Wood, and one day it was sold to a builder. Alas for the brownies and the rabbits, the birds and the little mice – they all had to leave when the trees were chopped down, and the wood made ready for houses to be built all over it!

The birds flew to another wood. The rabbits fled to the hillside a mile away. The little mice held a meeting, and decided to hide somewhere till the houses were built, and then become house-mice and live on food in the kitchens of the houses.

The brownies, too, held a meeting.

They were very tiny folk, these brownies, so small that you could easily hold six in your hand together. They were small enough to use a violet leaf for an umbrella, so you can guess how tiny they were.

"We will go to our cousins, who live in Wishing Wood," said the chief brownie, Chippy. "I know the way quite well. You go through the wood – down the lane – across the river – and up the hill. On the other side is Wishing Wood. It is a big place and there will be plenty of room for us to live there with our cousins."

So one night they set off. They ran through their own spoilt wood. They went down the lane, which seemed simply enormous to them. Then they came to the river.

But here they had to stop in dismay. They hadn't thought at all how they were to cross it! Now what were they to do?

"We haven't wings, so we can't fly," said Chippy.

"And there are no boats about," said Tiggy.

"Not even a leaf or two we could use as a raft," said Snippy.

"What shall we do?" said everyone together. "We *must* get across tonight!"

A rabbit popped his head out of a nearby hole. "What's the matter?" he said.

"Oh, can you help us?" asked the brownies, and they told the rabbit their trouble.

"No, I can't help you," said the rabbit, shaking his whiskery head. "But I know a very, very kind little boy called Billy, who lives in that house over there. He is very clever and *he* might help you. He once got me out of a trap. Go and knock at his window. He'll wake and do his best for you."

It was moonlight and the brownies could see the window that the rabbit pointed to. It had bars across, for it was a nursery window. They thanked the rabbit and ran to the garden hedge, crept through it and ran to the house. They climbed up the thick ivy, and stood on Billy's windowsill. By the moonlight that shone into the room they could quite well see Billy, fast asleep in his small bed.

Chippy tapped at the window. Billy stirred. Chippy tapped again. Billy sat up, wide awake. When he saw the brownies at the window he was too astonished to speak. Then he jumped out of bed and ran to let them in.

"Oh!" he said, "you dear little tiny creatures! I've always longed to see the little folk – and now I really have. I do hope I'm awake and not dreaming!"

"Oh, you're awake all right," said Chippy. "Listen, Billy! A rabbit told us you were clever and kind. Do you think you could help us?"

"I can try," said Billy, at once. "What do you want me to do?"

"Well," said Chippy, "we have to leave our home and we want to get to Wishing Wood, which is across the river and over the hill. We haven't wings to fly over the river, and we haven't boats. Could you tell us how to get across, please, Billy?"

Billy thought hard for a moment. "Let me see," he said. "It's no use lending you my ship – it's far too big.

And I've lost the oars of my little boat. And paper boats would soak with water and sink half-way across. Oh! I know! I've thought of just the right thing for you!"

"What? What?" cried the brownies excitedly.

"I'll make you walnut-shell boats!" said Billy. "They'll be just the right size for you. One of you will go nicely into each. They float beautifully – and I can make you tiny sails so that the wind will blow you across!"

Billy ran downstairs. He had counted the brownies and there were eleven of them. He took six walnuts from the dish of nuts on the dining-room sideboard.

He ran upstairs again. He carefully slit each walnut into its two half-shells and took out the nut. He and the brownies chewed the nuts between them as Billy worked.

"Now, there you are!" said Billy, when he had the six shells empty, standing neatly in their halves. "Twelve little boats! Good! Now I'll make the masts and the sails."

He got out a box in which he kept all sorts of odds and ends. In it were a lot of dead matches. Billy was not allowed to touch proper matches, only ones that had already been struck, but he had quite a lot of these.

He took out a dead match and made

holes in a small piece of white paper so that he could slip the bit of paper on the match for a sail! The match was the mast, you see. When he had got the sail nicely fixed, he looked for his tube of Seccotine.

"What's that?" asked the brownies in surprise, as they saw Billy squeezing a tiny, sticky sort of worm out of the tube on to the end of the match.

"It's Seccotine – sticky stuff that sticks things together," said Billy. "This drop of Seccotine will stick the end of the match to the bottom of the walnut shell, you see, brownies – and then you will have a nice straight mast, with a dear little sail to catch the wind!"

The brownies were simply amazed to see Billy making them the dear little walnut-shell boats. Billy was so quick and so clever!

He stuck the match into the bottom of a shell. He arranged the bit of paper for a sail. The boat was ready!

"One boat done," he said. "Now for the next!"

As soon as the brownies saw how the boats were made, they began to help. Tiggy got in a bit of a mess with the Seccotine, which stuck to his hands, and then everything seemed to stick to *him*! Poor Tiggy!

It was not long before there were twelve boats finished. "You only need eleven," said Billy, "but it would be quite a good idea to let the twelfth boat carry your bits of luggage. I can tie it on to one of the other boats."

Soon Billy and the brownies were creeping quietly down the garden to the river. Billy carried all the boats on a tiny tray, for fear of spoiling them. When he came to the river, he set the tray down on the ground.

He launched one tiny boat, and it bobbed up and down beautifully on the ripples. The wind pulled at the tiny sail. Billy carefully put a brownie in the boat, and away it went, bobbing merrily

over the river. Then another boat followed it – and another – and another – till the whole fleet was sailing away, looking perfectly lovely on the moonlit water.

The last but one had the twelfth luggage boat tied to the back of it. The two little boats bobbed safely away, the brownie in the first one waving goodbye. Billy stood and watched his fleet of walnut-shell boats sailing across to the other side, the wind blowing hard on the little paper sails. Not one boat sank.

"I do feel proud and pleased," said Billy to himself. "I've really done something tonight. I'll go to Wishing Wood some day and see if I can find those brownies again!"

He hasn't been yet, but I expect he will go soon. Would you like to make a fleet of walnut-shell boats like Billy? You can, easily. Sail them in the bath and they will look fine!